For Ellie

Don't Put Your Finger in the Jelly, Nelly!

Nick Sharratt

SCHOLASTIC

Don't put your finger
in the jelly,
Nelly!

You might upset a jellyphant!

Don't put your finger
in the pie,
Guy!

Don't put your finger
in the cheese,
Louise!

...You'll get caught by an alligator!

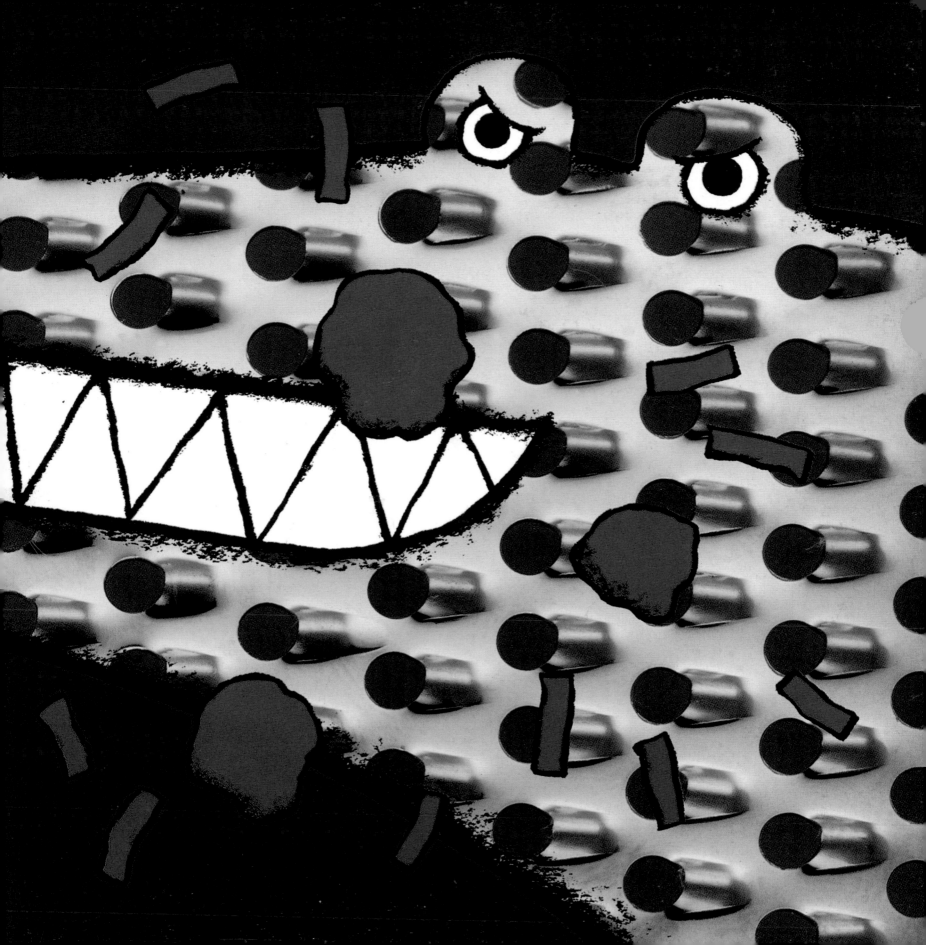

Don't put your finger
in the jam,
Sam!

Don't put your finger
in the pasta,
Jocasta!

Don't put your finger
in the shake,
Jake!

There's a
choctopus
about!

Don't put your finger
in there,
Claire!

THE
BAKER'S
SHOP

Unless you like doughnuts, that is!

Scholastic Children's Books
Euston House, 24 Eversholt Street
London NW1 1DB, UK
a division of Scholastic Ltd
London ~ New York ~ Toronto ~ Sydney ~ Auckland
Mexico City ~ New Delhi ~ Hong Kong

First published in 1993 by Scholastic Ltd
This enlarged paperback edition first published in 2006 by Scholastic Ltd

Copyright © Nick Sharratt, 1993

Photographs by Edgardo Braggio, Fotacha Ltd

ISBN: 978 0439 95062 6

Printed and bound in China

19 20

The right of Nick Sharratt to be identified as the author and illustrator of this work has been
asserted by him in accordance with the Copyright, Designs and Patents Act, 1988.

Papers used by Scholastic Children's Books are made from wood grown in sustainable forests.